a is for <del>apple</del> musk ox

erin cabatingan

illustrated by
matthew myers

A NEAL PORTER BOOK
ROARING BROOK PRESS
NEW YORK

Hey!
Hey you, Musk Ox!
Did you do this?
Did you eat
that apple?

Who me?
I can't remember.

Don’t lie!

Your mouth is full of apple.

Look! You’re drooling apple juice. How could you do that? You ruined my book.

Okay! So maybe I did eat it. But if I did, you should be thanking me.

I didn't ruin your book. I *saved* it. Every other alphabet book starts with "A is for apple." That's *sooo* boring. I think you should do something different. How about this:

A a is for apple

musk ox

That doesn't make sense.
Musk ox doesn't start with **A**.
It doesn't even
have **A** in it.

GLUE

Look, I'm tired of starting with **M**. I'm always
stuck in the middle. With all of those
letters on both sides, nobody
remembers me.

But musk ox does *not* start with A!

But musk oxen
are **awesome!**

Plus, we live in
the Arctic,
which includes
some of Alaska.

Fine. You can have **A**.
Let's just move on.

B is for baby

Baby? *Baby?*

Are you kidding me?
Who wants to look at
stinky babies in
dirty diapers?

I think babies
are cute.

Not as cute as musk oxen.
Here, let me fix that for you.

B is for baby

musk ox

That doesn't work. Musk ox doesn't start with **B**.

But our fur is **b**rown and **b**lack. It can also be white, but we're not at **W** yet.

Fine. *Fine.* Take **B**. In fact, why don't you take **C** as well?

C is for clown musk ox

Thank you, I will! Because musk oxen are **c**ool. Also, we live in **C**anada, too. I just didn't mention that before because we were talking about **A**.

d
d is for d<del>rum</del> musk ox

Because musk oxen are **d**aring.

e
e is for el~~egant~~ musk ox

Because musk oxen are **e**legant.

F f is for flowe̶
musk ox

Because musk oxen
have **f**ur. And lots
of it.
Does this **f**ur make
me look **f**at?

G g is for go̶o̶s̶e̶
musk ox

Because musk oxen eat **g**rass.
And live in **G**reenland.

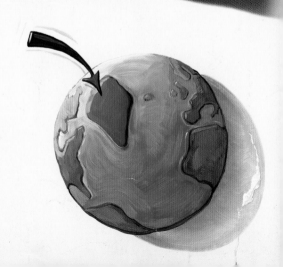

Hh

is for ~~house~~ musk ox

Because musk oxen have
horns and **h**ooves
and live in **h**erds.

Ii

is for ~~ink~~ musk ox

Because musk oxen are

~~intilijent~~
~~intalijunt~~
intelligent

J j is for jaguar joseph

Well, at least **Joseph**
starts with **J.**
I think the illustrator
messed up, though.

Naw, he didn't mess up.
That's me. My name is **Joseph.**
So really, **J** is for musk ox!

THE ARTIST'S OX

K is for kitten

musk ox

Because musk oxen are **k**ool!

Now wait just a minute, you can't do that. First of all, you already used cool. And second of all, you do not spell cool with a **K**.

Well you could.

No, you *couldn't*.

Could.

Couldn't!

Okay, fine. You can have **K**, too.

Thanks, dude.

Fine. **K** is for musk ox because musk oxen like to **k**ick anyone who disagrees with them.

L is for lamp

musk ox

Because musk oxen like

lollipops,

but only if they're grass-flavored.

Are lollipops ever grass-flavored?

No. What's your point?

M m is for musk ox

apple

Wait just a minute! Why isn't **M** for **m**usk ox? **M** should be for **m**usk ox! **M**usk ox starts with **M**!

Well, I felt kinda bad about what happened back at the beginning of the book, so I figured the apple could have **m**y spot.

But apple doesn't start with **M**.

Well, it is the **m**iddle of the apple.

That's called the apple *core*, not the apple **m**iddle.

Fine then. I **m**unched the apple. Plus, it was a **M**cIntosh. So there.

N

n is for naughty

musk ox

Because musk oxen are **n**ice.

Yeah, right.

O

O is for orange

musk ox

Because Eskimos call musk oxen **O**mingmak. It means "the animal with skin like a beard."

p is for pig wolf

Because wolves are **p**arty **p**oopers.

Are you just saying that
because wolves like
to eat musk oxen?

Maybe.

Q

q is for queen musk ox

Because the soft underwool of a musk ox is called Qiviut (kiv-ee-ute). That stuff keeps us warm in temperatures down to fifty degrees below zero. Brrrr!

R

r is for ~~rainbow~~ musk ox

Because musk oxen form **r**ings.

I'm **r**eally excited about this one. See, when a wolf is trying to eat one of us, we musk oxen form a **r**ing with all the calves in the middle. I'd like to see a wolf get past that **r**ing of horns. Hooah!

S is for ~~scarecrow~~ musk ox

Because musk oxen have **skirts**.

No, no, no!
Not that kind of **skirt**. Our long hair is sometimes called a **skirt**.

T **t** is for ~~turtle~~ **headache**

What? I don't get it.

Two male musk oxen,
twenty-five miles per hour
headbutts, ten, twelve,
sometimes twenty times?
Yeah, that's a headache.

Why do you
do that?

It's all for the ladies.

TV TOURNAMENT TO-NIGHT

U is for ~~umbrella~~ musk ox

Because musk oxen
have **u**nderwool!

You said that already.

Well, what do you want
me to say? Underwear?
Some parents might
not like that.

V is for valentine

musk ox

Because musk oxen are **v**ery!

Very what?

Very awesome, **v**ery cool,
very attractive: you can pick.

to Joseph
from Joseph

W

W is for ~~wagon~~ **musk ox**

Because musk oxen lived when
woolly mammoths were alive.

X

X is for ~~xylophone~~ **musk ox**

Because musk oxen look totally cool in **X**-rays.

Don't you think that's stretching it a bit?

Xellence 750

Well, it's not like we go around playing xylophones or anything.

Y is for musk ox

Because you would **y**ell and **y**ip
if you were being chased
by a rampaging musk ox.

(**Y**olanda, my **y**ounger sister)

Z
Z is for zebra

Finally
we agree on
something!

3 months old

Not really. I just wanted
to use this picture
of you.

What?
Where did you get that?

That's not me!

You know that's not me!

That's, uh, my sister.

Yeah! That's my sister.

e f g,

n o p!

w, x,

and Z!

Now you know why this book's cool.

It's because musk oxen rule!

Text copyright © 2012 by Erin Cabatingan

Illustrations copyright © 2012 by Matthew Myers

A Neal Porter Book

Published by Roaring Brook Press

Roaring Brook Press is a division of

Holtzbrinck Publishing Holdings Limited Partnership

175 Fifth Avenue, New York, New York 10010

mackids.com

Library of Congress Cataloging-in-Publication Data

Cabatingan, Erin.

  A is for musk ox / Erin Cabatingan ; illustrated by Matthew Myers. — 1st ed.

    p. cm.

  "A Neal Porter book."

  Summary: Musk Ox takes over an alphabet book, explaining to his friend Zebra

why almost every letter can be used to describe musk oxen.

  ISBN 978-1-59643-676-3 (alk. paper)

[1. Muskox—Fiction. 2. Zebras—Fiction. 3. Alphabet—Fiction. 4. Humorous stories.]

I. Myers, Matthew, 1960-- ill. II. Title.

  PZ7.C1073Aam 2012

  [E]—dc23

                       2011033794

Roaring Brook Press books are available for special promotions and premiums.

For details contact: Director of Special Markets, Holtzbrinck Publishers.

First edition 2012

Printed in China by Toppan Leefung Printing Ltd., Dongguan City, Guangdong Province

10   9   8   7   6   5   4   3   2   1

and musk ox

and musk ox

I can count higher than that